Ladybird Readers

The Zoo

Notes to teachers, parents, and carers

The *Ladybird Readers* Starter Level gently introduces children to the phonics approach to reading, by covering familiar themes that young readers will have studied (for example: colors, animals, and family).

Phonics focuses on how the individual sounds of letters are blended together to sound out a word. For example, /c/ /a/ /t/ when put together sound out the word **cat**.

The Starter Level is divided into two sub-level sections:
· **A** looks at simple words, such as **ant**, **dog**, and **red**.
· **B** explores trickier sound–letter combinations, such as the /**igh**/ sound in **night** and **fright**.

This book looks at the theme of **zoo animals** and focuses on these sounds and letters: **v w x z oo** (long) **i_e**

There are some activities to do in this book. They will help children practice these skills:

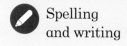 Spelling and writing    Speaking    Reading

LADYBIRD BOOKS
UK | USA | Canada | Ireland | Australia
India | New Zealand | South Africa
Ladybird Books is part of the Penguin Random House group of companies
whose addresses can be found at global.penguinrandomhouse.com.
www.penguin.co.uk   www.puffin.co.uk   www.ladybird.co.uk

First published 2017
003

Copyright © Ladybird Books Ltd, 2017
The moral rights of the author and illustrator have been asserted.

Printed in China

A CIP catalogue record for this book is available from the British Library

ISBN: 978-0-241-28346-2

All correspondence to Ladybird Books
Penguin Random House Childrens
80 Strand, London WC2R 0RL

Ladybird Readers

The Zoo

Look at the story

Series Editor: Sorrel Pitts
Story by Coleen Degnan-Veness
Illustrated by Ian Cunliffe

Picture words

Ella Elephant

Liz

Vick Vet

Zippy Zebra

lion

ox

Aa Bb Cc Dd Ee Ff Gg Hh Ii Jj Kk Ll Mm

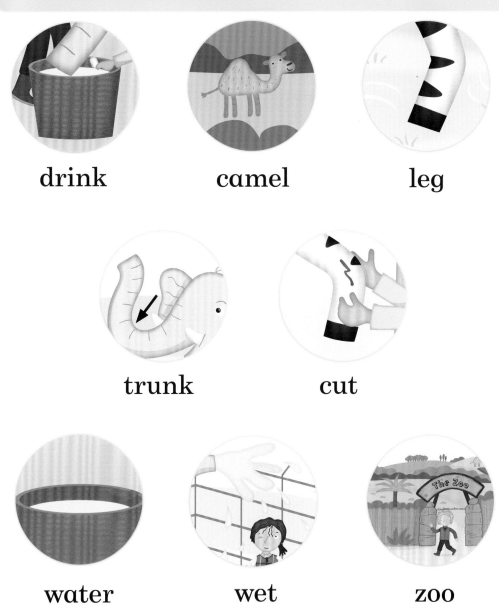

drink

camel

leg

trunk

cut

water

wet

zoo

Use these words to help you with the activity on page 16.

Vick Vet   Liz   lion

Vick

VICK 1

ox   camel   zoo

Zippy Zebra

leg

cut

Vick Vet

Liz

Ella Elephant

water

drink

trunk

Vick Vet

14

wet

15

Activity

1 **Say the sounds. Read the words. Circle the word that is different.**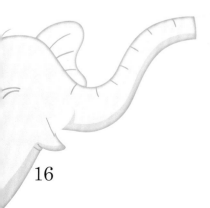

    1   **w**   water   (Vick)   wet

    2   **v**   Vick   vet   white

    3   **z**   zebra   Zippy   ox

    4   **e**   happy   Ella   elephant

The Zoo

Read the story

Vick Vet drives to the zoo.
Liz likes her job at the zoo.

The camel, the ox, and the lions like her, too!

Zippy Zebra is black and white. He has a bad leg.

Vick Vet opens a door.
She puts Zippy in this pen.

Zippy has a cut on his leg.

Zippy is happy.

I can help Zippy.

Liz and Vick Vet go to
Ella Elephant. Ella Elephant
has a gray body.

Ella drinks the water
with her trunk.

Ella's trunk is above
Vick Vet's head.

Vick Vet is wet from head to foot!

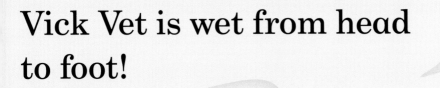

Ella is enjoying this!

Activities

2   Look. Say the words. Match.

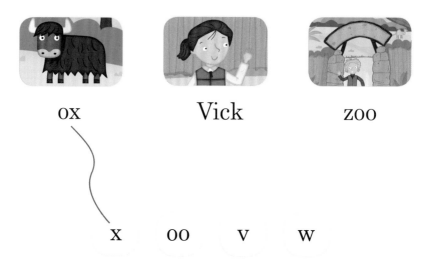

ox   Vick   zoo

x   oo   v   w

vet   water   wet

3 **Look. Say the words.**
Put a ☑ **or a** ☒ **in the boxes.**

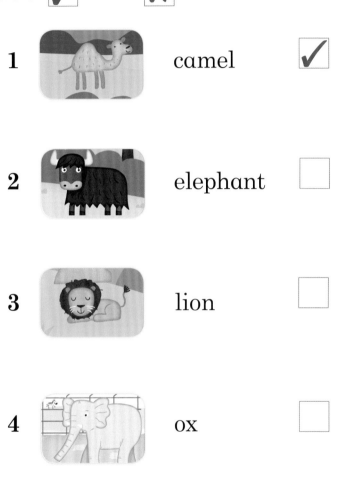

1   camel   ✓

2   elephant

3   lion

4   ox

5   zebra

4 Look. Write the letters. Say the words. ✏️ 💬

(i) (e)

1 L _i_ z

2 dr _____ v _____

3 V _____ ck

4 v _____ t

5 w _____ t

5 **Read the words. Color names in red. Color animals in blue. Then, find the words.**

elephant

Vick

ox

Liz

zebra

d g z e b r a p n e l e p h a n t f x V i c k c h o x b o L i z

Starter Level A and B

The Zoo

978–0–241–28346–2 ☐

Dom Dog and his Boat

978–0–241–28340–0 ☐

Ted in Bed

978–0–241–28342–4 ☐

The Fun Run

978–0–241–28343–1 ☐

Brother Blue

978–0–241–28338–7 ☐

Doctor Panda

978–0–241–28339–4 ☐

Farmer Carl

978–0–241–28341–7 ☐

The Old Boat

978–0–241–28345–5 ☐